THE CHOCOLATE BOX

BY

AGATHA CHRISTIE

LONDON
JOHN LANE THE BODLEY HEAD LIMITED
First published in Great Britain in May 23, 1923

THE CHOCOLATE BOX

It was a wild night. Outside, the wind howled malevolently, and the rain beat against the windows in great gusts.

Poirot and I sat facing the hearth, our legs stretched out to the cheerful blaze. Between us was a small table. On my side of it stood some carefully brewed hot toddy; on Poirot's was a cup of thick, rich chocolate which I would not have drunk for a hundred pounds! Poirot sipped the thick brown mess in the pink china cup, and sighed with contentment.

'Quelle belle vie!' he murmured.

'Yes, it's a good old world,' I agreed. 'Here am I with a job, and a good job too! And here are you, famous -'

'Oh, mon ami!' protested Poirot.

'But you are. And rightly so! When I think back on your long line of successes, I am positively amazed. I don't believe you know what failure is!'

'He would be a droll kind of original who could say that!'

'No, but seriously, have you ever failed?'

'Innumerable times, my friend. What would you? La bonne chance, it cannot always be on your side. I have been called in too late. Very often another, working towards the same goal, has arrived there first. Twice have I been stricken down with illness just as I was on the point of success. One must take the downs with the ups, my friend.'

'I didn't quite mean that,' I said. 'I meant, had you ever been completely down and out over a case through your own fault?'

'Ah, I comprehend! You ask if I have ever made the complete prize ass of myself, as you say over here? Once, my friend -' A slow, reflective smile hovered over his face. 'Yes, once I made a fool of myself.'

He sat up suddenly in his chair.

'See here, my friend, you have, I know, kept a record of my little successes. You shall add one more story to the collection, the story of a failure!'

He leaned forward and placed a log on the fire. Then, after carefully wiping his hands on a little duster that hung on a nail by the fireplace, he leaned back and commenced his story.

That of which I tell you (said M. Poirot) took place in Belgium many years ago. It was at the time of the terrible struggle in France between church and state. M. Paul Déroulard was a French deputy of note. It was an open secret that the portfolio of a Minister awaited him. He was among the bitterest of the anti-Catholic party, and it was certain that on his accession to power, he would have to face violent enmity. He was in many ways a peculiar man. Though he neither drank nor smoked, he was nevertheless not so scrupulous in other ways. You comprehend, Hastings, c'était des femmes - toujours des femmes!

He had married some years earlier a young lady from Brussels who had brought him a substantial dot. Undoubtedly the money was useful to him in his career, as his family was not rich, though on the other hand he was entitled to call himself M. le Baron if he chose. There were no children of the marriage, and his wife died after two years - the result of a fall downstairs. Among the property which she bequeathed to him was a house on the Avenue Louise in Brussels.

It was in this house that his sudden death took place, the event coinciding with the resignation of the Minister whose portfolio he was to inherit. All the papers printed long notices of his career. His death, which had taken place quite suddenly in the evening after dinner, was attributed to heart-failure.

At that time, mon ami, I was, as you know, a member of the Belgian detective force. The death of M. Paul Déroulard was not particularly interesting to me. I am, as you also know, bon catholique, and his demise seemed to me fortunate.

It was some three days afterwards, when my vacation had just begun, that I received a visitor at my own apartments - a lady, heavily veiled, but evidently quite young; and I perceived at once that she was a jeune fille tout à fait comme il faut.

'You are Monsieur Hercule Poirot?' she asked in a low sweet voice.

I bowed.

'Of the detective service?'

Again I bowed. 'Be seated, I pray of you, mademoiselle,' I said.

She accepted a chair and drew aside her veil. Her face was charming, though marred with tears, and haunted as though with some poignant anxiety.

'Monsieur,' she said, 'I understand that you are now taking a vacation. Therefore you will be free to take up a private case. You understand that I do not wish to call in the police.'

I shook my head. 'I fear what you ask is impossible, mademoiselle. Even though on vacation, I am still of the police.'

She leaned forward. 'Ecoutez, monsieur. All that I ask of you is to investigate. The result of your investigations you are at perfect liberty to report to the police. If what I believe to be true is true, we shall need all the machinery of the law.'

That placed a somewhat different complexion on the matter, and I placed myself at her service without more ado.

A slight colour rose in her cheeks. 'I thank you, monsieur. It is the death of M. Paul Déroulard that I ask you to investigate.'

'Comment?' I exclaimed, surprised.

'Monsieur, I have nothing to go upon - nothing but my woman's instinct, but I am convinced - convinced, I tell you - that M. Déroulard did not die a natural death!'

'But surely the doctors -'

'Doctors may be mistaken. He was so robust, so strong. Ah, Monsieur Poirot, I beseech of you to help me -'

The poor child was almost beside herself. She would have knelt to me. I soothed her as best I could.

'I will help you, mademoiselle. I feel almost sure that your fears are unfounded, but we will see. First, I will ask you to describe to me the inmates of the house.'

'There are the domestics, of course, Jeanette, Félicie, and Denise the cook. She has been there many years; the others are simple country girls. Also there is François, but he too is an old servant. Then there is Monsieur Déroulard's mother who lived with him, and myself. My name is Virginie Mesnard. I am a poor cousin of the late Madame Déroulard, M. Paul's wife, and I have been a member of their ménage for over three years. I have now described to you the household. There were also two guests staying in the house.'

'And they were?'

'M. de Saint Alard, a neighbour of M. Déroulard's in France. Also an English friend, Mr John Wilson.'

'Are they still with you?'

'Mr Wilson, yes, but M. de Saint Alard departed yesterday.'

'And what is your plan, Mademoiselle Mesnard?'

'If you will present yourself at the house in half an hour's time, I will have arranged some story to account for your presence. I had better represent you to be connected with journalism in some way. I shall say you have come from Paris, and that you have brought a card of introduction from M. de Saint Alard. Madame Déroulard is very feeble in health, and will pay little attention to details.'

On mademoiselle's ingenious pretext I was admitted to the house, and after a brief interview with the dead deputy's mother, who was a wonderfully imposing and aristocratic figure though obviously in failing health, I was made free of the premises.

I wonder, my friend (continued Poirot), whether you can possibly figure to yourself the difficulties of my task? Here was a man whose death had taken place three days previously. If there had been foul play, only one possibility was admittable - poison! And I had had no chance of seeing the body, and there was no possibility of examining, or analysing, any medium in which the poison could have been administered. There were no clues, false or otherwise, to consider. Had the man been poisoned? Had he died a natural death? I, Hercule Poirot, with nothing to help me, had to decide.

First, I interviewed the domestics, and with their aid, I recapitulated the evening. I paid especial notice to the food at dinner, and the method of serving it. The soup had been served by M. Déroulard himself from a tureen. Next a dish of cutlets, then a chicken. Finally a compote of fruits. And all placed on the table, and served by Monsieur himself. The coffee was brought in a big pot to the dinner-table. Nothing there, mon ami - impossible to poison one without poisoning all!

After dinner Madame Déroulard had retired to her own apartments and Mademoiselle Virginie had accompanied her. The three men had adjourned to M. Déroulard's study. Here they had chatted amicably for some time, when suddenly, without any warning, the deputy had fallen heavily to the ground. M. de Saint Alard had rushed out and told François to fetch a doctor immediately. He said it was without doubt an apoplexy, explained the man. But when the doctor arrived, the patient was past help.

Mr John Wilson, to whom I was presented by Mademoiselle Virginie, was what was known in those days as a regular John Bull Englishman, middle-aged and burly. His account, delivered in very British French, was substantially the same.

'Déroulard went very red in the face, and down he fell.'

There was nothing further to be found out there. Next I went to the scene of the tragedy, the study, and was left alone there at my own request. So far there was nothing to support Mademoiselle Mesnard's theory. I could not but believe that it was a delusion on her part. Evidently she had entertained a romantic passion for the dead man which had not permitted her to take a normal view of the case. Nevertheless, I searched the study with meticulous care. It was just possible that a hypodermic needle might have been introduced into the dead man's chair in such a way as to allow of a fatal injection. The minute puncture it would cause was likely to remain unnoticed. But I could discover no sign to support that theory. I flung myself down in the chair with a gesture of despair.

'Enfin, I abandon it!' I said aloud. 'There is not a clue anywhere! Everything is perfectly normal.'

As I said the words, my eyes fell on a large box of chocolates standing on a table near by, and my heart gave a leap. It might not be a clue to M. Déroulard's death, but here at least was something that was not normal. I lifted the lid. The box was full, untouched; not a chocolate was missing - but that only made the peculiarity that had caught my eye more striking. For, see you, Hastings, while the box itself was pink, the lid was blue. Now, one often sees a blue ribbon on a pink box, and vice versa, but a box of one colour, and a lid of another - no; decidedly - ça ne se voit jamais!

I did not as yet see that this little incident was of any use to me, yet I determined to investigate it as being out of the ordinary. I rang the bell for François, and asked him if his late master had been fond of sweets. A faint melancholy smile came to his lips.

'Passionately fond of them, monsieur. He would always have a box of chocolates in the house. He did not drink wine of any kind, you see.'

'Yet this box has not been touched?' I lifted the lid to show him.

'Pardon, monsieur, but that was a new box purchased on the day of his death, the other being nearly finished.'

'Then the other box was finished on the day of his death,' I said slowly.

'Yes, monsieur, I found it empty in the morning and threw it away.'

'Did M. Déroulard eat sweets at all hours of the day?'

'Usually after dinner, monsieur.'

I began to see light.

'François,' I said, 'you can be discreet?'

'If there is need, monsieur.'

'Bon! Know, then, that I am of the police. Can you find me that other box?'

'Without doubt, monsieur. It will be in the dustbin.'

He departed, and returned in a few minutes with a dust-covered object. It was the duplicate of the box I held, save for the fact that this time the box was blue and the lid was pink. I thanked François, recommended him once more to be discreet, and left the house in the Avenue Louise without more ado.

Next day I called upon the doctor who had attended M. Déroulard. With him I had a difficult task. He entrenched himself prettily behind a wall of learned phraseology, but I fancied that he was not quite as sure about the case as he would like to be.

'There have been many curious occurrences of the kind,' he observed, when I had managed to disarm him somewhat. 'A sudden fit of anger, a violent emotion - after a heavy dinner, c'est entendu - then, with an access of rage, the blood flies to the head, and pst! - there you are!'

'But M. Déroulard had had no violent emotion.'

'No? I made sure that he had been having a stormy altercation with M. de Saint Alard.'

'Why should he?'

'C'est évident!' The doctor shrugged his shoulders. 'Was not M. de Saint Alard a Catholic of the most fanatical? Their friendship was being ruined by this question of church and state. Not a day passed without discussions. To M. de Saint Alard, Déroulard appeared almost as Antichrist.'

This was unexpected, and gave me food for thought.

'One more question, Doctor: would it be possible to introduce a fatal dose of poison into a chocolate?'

'It would be possible, I suppose,' said the doctor slowly. 'Pure prussic acid would meet the case if there were no chance of evaporation, and a tiny globule of anything might be swallowed unnoticed - but it does not seem a very likely supposition. A chocolate full of morphine or strychnine -' He made a wry face. 'You comprehend, M. Poirot - one bite would be enough! The unwary one would not stand upon ceremony.'

'Thank you, M. le Docteur.'

I withdrew. Next I made inquiries of the chemists, especially those in the neighbourhood of the Avenue Louise. It is good to be of the police. I got the information I wanted without any trouble. Only in one case could I hear of any poison having been supplied to the house in question. This was some eye drops of atropine sulphate for Madame Déroulard. Atropine is a potent poison, and for the moment I was elated, but the symptoms of atropine poisoning are closely allied to those of ptomaine, and bear no resemblance to those I was studying. Besides, the prescription was an old one. Madame Déroulard had suffered from cataract in both eyes for many years.

I was turning away discouraged when the chemist's voice called me back.

'Un moment, M. Poirot. I remember, the girl who brought that prescription, she said something about having to go on to the English chemist. You might try there.'

I did. Once more enforcing my official status, I got the information I wanted. On the day before M. Déroulard's death they had made up a prescription for Mr John Wilson. Not that there was any making up about it. They were simply little tablets of trinitrine. I asked if I might see some. He showed me them, and my heart beat faster - for the tiny tablets were of chocolate.

'It is a poison?' I asked.

'No, monsieur.'

'Can you describe to me its effect?'

'It lowers the blood-pressure. It is given for some forms of heart trouble - angina pectoris for instance. It relieves the arterial tension. In arteriosclerosis -'

I interrupted him. 'Ma foi! This rigmarole says nothing to me. Does it cause the face to flush?'

'Certainly it does.'

'And supposing I ate ten - twenty of your little tablets, what then?'

'I should not advise you to attempt it,' he replied drily.

'And yet you say it is not poison?'

'There are many things not called poison which can kill a man,' he replied as before.

I left the shop elated. At last, things had begun to march!

I now knew that John Wilson held the means for the crime - but what about the motive? He had come to Belgium on business, and had asked M. Déroulard, whom he knew slightly, to put him up. There was apparently no way in which Déroulard's death could benefit him. Moreover, I discovered by inquiries in England that he had suffered for some years from that painful form of heart disease known as angina. Therefore he had a genuine right to have those tablets in his possession. Nevertheless, I was convinced that someone had gone to the chocolate box, opening the full one first by mistake, and had abstracted the contents of the last chocolate, cramming in instead as many little trinitrin tablets as it would hold. The chocolates were large ones. Between twenty or thirty tablets, I felt sure, could have been inserted. But who had done this?

There were two guests in the house. John Wilson had the means. Saint Alard had the motive. Remember, he was a fanatic, and there is no fanatic like a religious fanatic. Could he, by any means, have got hold of John Wilson's trinitrine?

Another little idea came to me. Ah! You smile at my little ideas! Why had Wilson run out of trinitrine? Surely he would bring an adequate supply from England. I called once more at the house in the Avenue Louise. Wilson was out, but I saw the girl who did his room, Félicie. I demanded of her immediately whether it was not true that M. Wilson had lost a bottle from his washstand some little time ago. The girl responded eagerly. It was quite true. She, Félicie, had been blamed for it. The English gentleman had evidently thought that she had broken it, and did not like to say so. Whereas she had never even touched it. Without doubt it was Jeannette - always nosing round where she had no business to be -

I calmed the flow of words, and took my leave. I knew now all that I wanted to know. It remained for me to prove my case. That, I felt, would not be easy. I might be sure that Saint Alard had removed the bottle of trinitrine from John Wilson's washstand, but to convince others, I would have to produce evidence. And I had none to produce!

Never mind. I knew - that was the great thing. You remember our difficulty in the Styles case, Hastings? There again, I knew but it took me a long time to find the last link which made my chain of evidence against the murderer complete.

I asked for an interview with Mademoiselle Mesnard. She came at once. I demanded of her the address of M. de Saint Alard. A look of trouble came over her face.

'Why do you want it, monsieur?'

'Mademoiselle, it is necessary.'

She seemed doubtful - troubled.

'He can tell you nothing. He is a man whose thoughts are not in this world. He hardly notices what goes on around him.'

'Possibly, mademoiselle. Nevertheless, he was an old friend of M. Déroulard's. There may be things he can tell me - things of the past - old grudges - old love-affairs.'

The girl flushed and bit her lip. 'As you please - but - but - I feel sure now that I have been mistaken. It was good of you to accede to my demand, but I was upset - almost distraught at the time. I see now that there is no mystery to solve. Leave it, I beg of you, monsieur.'

I eyed her closely.

'Mademoiselle,' I said, 'it is sometimes difficult for a dog to find a scent, but once he has found it, nothing on earth will make him leave it! That is if he is a good dog! And I, mademoiselle, I, Hercule Poirot, am a very good dog.'

Without a word she turned away. A few minutes later she returned with the address written on a sheet of paper. I left the house. François was waiting for me outside. He looked at me anxiously.

'There is no news, monsieur?'

'None as yet, my friend.'

'Ah! Pauvre Monsieur Déroulard!' he sighed. 'I too was of his way of thinking. I do not care for priests. Not that I would say so in the house. The women are all devout - a good thing perhaps. Madame est très pieuse - et Mademoiselle Virginie aussi.'

Mademoiselle Virginie? Was she 'très pieuse?' Thinking of the tear-stained passionate face I had seen that first day, I wondered.

Having obtained the address of M. de Saint Alard, I wasted no time. I arrived in the neighbourhood of his château in the Ardennes but it was some days before I could find a pretext for gaining admission to the house. In the end I did - how do you think - as a plumber, mon ami! It was the affair of a moment to arrange a neat little gas leak in his bedroom. I departed for my tools, and took care to return with them at an hour when I knew I should have the field pretty well to myself. What I was searching for, I hardly knew. The one thing needful, I could not believe there was any chance of finding. He would never have run the risk of keeping it.

Still when I found a little cupboard above the washstand locked, I could not resist the temptation of seeing what was inside it. The lock was quite a simple one to pick. The door swung open. It was full of old bottles. I took them up one by one with a trembling hand. Suddenly, I uttered a cry. Figure to yourself, my friend, I held in my hand a little phial with an English chemist's label. On it were the words: 'Trinitrine Tablets. One to be taken when required. Mr John Wilson.'

I controlled my emotion, closed the little cupboard, slipped the bottle into my pocket, and continued to repair the gas leak! One must be methodical. Then I left the château, and took train for my own country as soon as possible. I arrived in Brussels late that night. I was writing out a report for the préfet in the morning, when a note was brought to me. It was from old Madame Déroulard, and it summoned me to the house in the Avenue Louise without delay.

François opened the door to me.

'Madame la Baronne is awaiting you.'

He conducted me to her apartments. She sat in state in a large armchair. There was no sign of Mademoiselle Virginie.

'M. Poirot,' said the old lady. 'I have just learned that you are not what you pretend to be. You are a police officer.'

'That is so, madame.'

'You came here to inquire into the circumstances of my son's death?'

Again I replied: 'That is so, madame.'

'I should be glad if you would tell me what progress you have made.'

I hesitated.

'First I would like to know how you have learned all this, madame.'

'From one who is no longer of this world.'

Her words, and the brooding way she uttered them, sent a chill to my heart. I was incapable of speech.

'Wherefore, monsieur, I would beg of you most urgently to tell me exactly what progress you have made in your investigation.'

'Madame, my investigation is finished.'

'My son?'

'Was killed deliberately.'

'You know by whom?'

'Yes, madame.'

'Who, then?'

'M. de Saint Alard.'

The old lady shook her head.

'You are wrong. M. de Saint Alard is incapable of such a crime.'

'The proofs are in my hands.'

'I beg of you once more to tell me all.'

This time I obeyed, going over each step that had led me to the discovery of the truth. She listened attentively. At the end she nodded her head.

'Yes, yes, it is all as you say, all but one thing. It was not M. de Saint Alard who killed my son. It was I, his mother.'

I stared at her. She continued to nod her head gently.

'It is well that I sent for you. It is the providence of the good God that Virginie told me before she departed for the convent, what she had done. Listen, M. Poirot! My son was an evil man. He persecuted the church. He led a life of mortal sin. He dragged down other souls beside his own. But there was worse than that. As I came out of my room in this house one morning, I saw my daughter-in-law standing at the head of the stairs. She was reading a letter. I saw my son steal up behind her. One swift push, and she fell, striking her head on the marble steps. When they picked her up she was dead. My son was a murderer, and only I, his mother, knew it.'

She closed her eyes for a moment. 'You cannot conceive, monsieur, of my agony, my despair. What was I to do? Denounce him to the police? I could not bring myself to do it. It was my duty, but my flesh was weak. Besides, would they believe me? My eyesight had been failing for some time - they would say I was mistaken. I kept silence. But my conscience gave me no peace. By keeping silence I too was a murderer. My son inherited his wife's money. He flourished as the green bay tree. And now he was to have a Minister's portfolio. His persecution of the church would be redoubled. And there was Virginie. She, poor child, beautiful, naturally pious, was fascinated by him. He had a strange and terrible power over women. I saw it coming. I was powerless to prevent it. He had no intention of marrying her. The time came when she was ready to yield everything to him.

'Then I saw my path clear. He was my son. I had given him life. I was responsible for him. He had killed one woman's body, now he would kill another's soul! I went to Mr Wilson's room, and took the bottle of tablets. He had once said laughingly that there were enough in it to kill a man! I went into the study and opened the big box of chocolates that always stood on the table. I opened a new box by mistake. The other was on the table also. There was just one chocolate left in it. That simplified things. No one ate chocolates except my son and Virginie. I would keep her with me that night. All went as I had planned -'

She paused, closing her eyes a minute then opened them again.

'M. Poirot, I am in your hands. They tell me I have not many days to live. I am willing to answer for my action before the good God. Must I answer for it on earth also?'

I hesitated. 'But the empty bottle, madame,' I said to gain time. 'How came that into M. de Saint Alard's possession?'

'When he came to say goodbye to me, monsieur, I slipped it into his pocket. I did not know how to get rid of it. I am so infirm that I cannot move about much without help, and finding it empty in my rooms might have caused suspicion. You understand, monsieur -' she drew herself up to her full height - 'it was with no idea of casting suspicion on M. de Saint Alard! I never dreamed of such a thing. I thought his valet would find an empty bottle and throw it away without question.'

I bowed my head. 'I comprehend, madame,' I said.

'And your decision, monsieur?'

Her voice was firm and unfaltering, her head held as high as ever. I rose to my feet.

'Madame,' I said, 'I have the honour to wish you good day. I have made my investigations - and failed! The matter is closed.'

He was silent for a moment, then said quietly: 'She died just a week later. Mademoiselle Virginie passed through her novitiate, and duly took the veil. That, my friend, is the story. I must admit that I do not make a fine figure in it.'

'But that was hardly a failure,' I expostulated. 'What else could you have thought under the circumstances?'

'Ah, sacré, mon ami,' cried Poirot, becoming suddenly animated. 'Is it that you do not see? But I was thirty-six times an idiot! My grey cells, they functioned not at all. The whole time I had the true clue in my hands.'

'What clue?'

'The chocolate box! Do you not see? Would anyone in possession of their full eyesight make such a mistake? I knew Madame Déroulard had cataract - the atropine drops told me that. There was only one person in the household whose eyesight was such that she could not see which lid to replace. It was the chocolate box that started me on the track, and yet up to the end I failed consistently to perceive its real significance!

'Also my psychology was at fault. Had M. de Saint Alard been the criminal, he would never have kept an incriminating bottle. Finding it was a proof of his innocence. I had learned already from Mademoiselle Virginie that he was absent-minded. Altogether it was a miserable affair that I have recounted to you there! Only to you have I told the story. You comprehend, I do not figure well in it! An old lady commits a crime in such a simple and clever fashion that I, Hercule Poirot, am completely deceived. Sapristi! It does not bear thinking of! Forget it. Or no - remember it, and if you think at any time that I am growing conceited - it is not likely, but it might arise.'

I concealed a smile.

'Eh bien, my friend, you shall say to me, "Chocolate box". Is it agreed?'

'It's a bargain!'

'After all,' said Poirot reflectively, 'it was an experience! I, who have undoubtedly the finest brain in Europe at present, can afford to be magnanimous!'

'Chocolate box,' I murmured gently.

'Pardon, mon ami?'

I looked at Poirot's innocent face, as he bent forward inquiringly, and my heart smote me. I had suffered often at his hands, but I, too, though not possessing the finest brain in Europe, could afford to be magnanimous!

'Nothing,' I lied, and lit another pipe, smiling to myself.

THE END

Made in United States
North Haven, CT
10 June 2024

53453083R00017